Disney's
My Very First Winnie the Pooh™

Pooh's Neighborhood

Kathleen W. Zoehfeld Illustrated by Robbin Cuddy

SCHOLASTIC INC.
New York Toronto London Auckland Sydney

12 11 10 9 8 7 6 5 4 3 2 1   8 9/9 0 1 2 3/0

Printed in the U.S.A.   24
First Scholastic printing, October 1998

Disney's
My Very First Winnie the Pooh
Pooh's Neighborhood

"**I** say, it's a splendid day in the neighborhood!" said Owl.

"It's a nice day here, too," said Winnie the Pooh.

"Exactly what I'm saying," said Owl, "a perfectly splendid day in the neighborhood."

"Which neighbor wood are we talking about?" asked Pooh.

"Neighbor*hood*," said Owl. "*Our* neighborhood— the place where we live and where all our neighbors live and are neighborly."

"Oh," said Pooh, "it *is* a splendid day in it, isn't it?"

"Quite," said Owl. "Now I'm off for an owl's-eye view!" He flew up and circled once around Pooh's house.

"What does it look like from up there?" called Pooh.

"I can see the Hundred-Acre Wood spread out below me," said Owl. "And it's a fine place, indeed."

As Owl flew off, Pooh began to think about what it means to live in a neighborhood, and he thought perhaps he would bring a neighborly present to his closest neighbor, Piglet.

He took a honeypot out of his cupboard and tied a nice blue ribbon around it.

Then he tucked it comfortably under his arm and stumped down the path toward Piglet's house. But when he reached his Thoughtful Spot, which is halfway between his house and Piglet's, Pooh suddenly had a thought: I *could* take this path straight to Piglet's house. Or—I could go up the path and around the whole neighborhood. And sooner or later the path would take me to Piglet's house, anyway.

And that is what he did.

After he had walked for a time, he came to the house where Kanga and Roo live.

"Hello, Kanga," said Pooh. "I'm just on my way to deliver this neighborly present to Piglet."

"But, Pooh dear, Piglet lives that way," said Kanga, pointing down the very path by which Pooh had come.

"Yes," said Pooh, "but today I'm going the long way."

"Oh, I see," said Kanga. "In that case, perhaps you should join us for a snack."

"Come on, Pooh!" cried Roo. "We're going to the picnic spot."

Pooh said he *was* feeling a bit eleven o'clockish; so they all went together, past the Sandy Pit Where Roo Plays, up to the picnic spot to share a little something.

Half an hour—and one picnic basket—later, Pooh thanked Kanga, tucked Piglet's honeypot back under his arm, and stumped down the path toward Rabbit's house.

"Hello, Rabbit!" called Pooh. "I'm on my way to Piglet's to give him this neighborly present."

"If you're going to Piglet's house, what are you doing here?" asked Rabbit.

"I'm going the long way," said Pooh.

"More like the *wrong* way, if you ask me," said  Rabbit. "But since you're here, would you mind taking these carrots to Christopher Robin? I promised he'd have them in time for lunch."

Well, at the mention of the word "lunch," Pooh noticed that his tummy was feeling just the tiniest bit rumbly.

"I'd be happy to," he said.

With carrots under one arm and honeypot under the other, he walked along until he came to the place where the stepping-stones cross the stream.

"One, two, three, four," he counted as he teetered from stone to stone. Eight or nine of Rabbit's friends and relations heard Pooh and peeked out their windows and doors.

Pooh shouted, "Halloo!"

Rabbit's friends and relations waved.

Pooh marched across open slopes of heather and up steep banks of sandstone until at last, tired and hungry, he arrived at Christopher Robin's door.

"Oh, my carrots!" cried Christopher Robin happily. "Thank you for delivering them."

"It seemed the neighborly thing to do," said Pooh proudly.

"Would you like to join me for lunch?" Christopher Robin asked.

And Pooh said, "Well, I really am on my way to Piglet's to bring him this present. But I don't see why I couldn't stop, just for a little while."

After lunch, and a longish snooze, Pooh was back on his way.

He walked down the path through the Little
Pine Wood and climbed over the gate into
Eeyore's Gloomy Place,
which was where
Eeyore lived.

"Hello, Eeyore," said
Pooh. "I was just on my
way to Piglet's house
with this neighborly present—"

"Not coming to visit me," said Eeyore. "I didn't
think so. It's been such a busy week already.
Why, only four days ago Tigger bounced me on
his way to the swimming hole. How many
visitors can you expect, really?"

And Pooh, feeling rather badly now, offered Eeyore a nice lick of honey.

Pooh opened the jar, and Eeyore peered in. He looked back up at Pooh.

Pooh peered in. "Empty," he said.

"That's what it looked like to me," said Eeyore.

"Oh bother," said Pooh.

He stumped off glumly, trying to think how he was going to tell Piglet about the neighborly present Piglet was not going to get.

Pooh had almost arrived at the Place Where the Woozle Wasn't and was deciding to take the long path around it, just in case the woozle was, when he saw Owl flying over.

"I've seen our whole neighborhood today," Pooh told him. "But now I have no neighborly present left for Piglet."

"The bees have been quite busy at the old bee tree lately," said Owl. "Perhaps you can get a fill-up there."

"That's a good idea, Owl, but it's such a long way," sighed Pooh.

"Come along," said Owl. "We'll take the shortcut through the woods."

So they walked together until they came to an open place in the middle of the forest, and in the middle of this place was the old bee tree. Pooh could hear a loud buzzing near the top.

Up, up, up he climbed.

"Go up higher!" called Owl. "Past the bees. To the very top of the tree. Now, look all around you. What do you see?"

The Hundred-Acre Wood was spread out below him.

"Our neighborhood!" cried Pooh. "Our beautiful home!"

"That's the owl's-eye view," said Owl grandly.

"Oh, I can see poor Piglet out sweeping his walk," said Pooh. "Looks like he could use some company."

Nice Place for Picnics

Pooh's House

Sandy Pit Where Roo Plays

POOH'S THOTFUL SPOT

Piglet's House

HUNDRED-ACRE WOOD

Rabbit's
House

anga and
oo's House

Rabbit's
Friends and
Relations

Christopher
Robin's
House

ee
ee

Owl's
House

Where the
oozle Wasn't

Eeyore's
Gloomy
Place

So Pooh filled the honeypot once more, and he and Owl went to Piglet's house for supper.